DATE DUE

NOV 8 2011		
JAN 0 4 2012	JAN 0 6 2016	
JAN 2 7 2012	SEP 3 0 2016	
SEP 2 1 2012		
NOV 1 5 2012		
SEP 2 7 2013		
OCT 2 9 2013		

Demco, Inc. 38-293

The Thing in the Woods

by Steve Brezenoff

illustrated by Richard Pellegrino

Librarian Reviewer
Marci Peschke
Librarian, Dallas Independent School District
MA Education Reading Specialist, Stephen F. Austin State University
Learning Resources Endorsement, Texas Women's University

Reading Consultant
Elizabeth Stedem
Educator/Consultant, Colorado Springs, CO
MA in Elementary Education, University of Denver, CO

STONE ARCH BOOKS
www.stonearchbooks.com

Shade Books are published by Stone Arch Books,
A Capstone Imprint
151 Good Counsel Drive, P.O. Box 669
Mankato, Minnesota 56002
www.capstonepub.com

Library of Congress Cataloging-in-Publication Data
Brezenoff, Steven.
    The Thing in the Woods / by Steve Brezenoff; illustrated by
Richard Pellegrino.
        p. cm. — (Shade Books)
        ISBN 978-1-4342-0795-1 (library binding)
        ISBN 978-1-4342-0891-0 (pbk.)
        [1. Camping—Fiction. 2. Supernatural—Fiction.] I. Pellegrino,
Richard, 1980- ill. II. Title.
PZ7.B7576Th 2009
[Fic]—dc22   2008008007

Summary: The ghost story Jason's dad told him is coming true!

Art Director: Heather Kindseth
Graphic Designer: Kay Fraser

Printed in the United States of America in Stevens Point, Wisconsin.
012010
005677R

TABLE OF CONTENTS

CHAPTER 1

Car Trouble

A single drop of sweat slid down Jason's nose. He crossed his eyes to watch it as it fell. It hissed as it hit the surface of the rock Jason was sitting on.

"Dad," Jason said. "It's too hot!"

"I know, Jay," his dad replied. He took some gear out of the trunk of their car. He pulled off his straw cowboy hat and wiped the sweat from his forehead.

"The sun will set soon," Dad said. He put his hat back on. "You'll be shocked by how cold it can get out here at night," he added. "You'll be freezing."

Jason shook his head. "No way," he said. "I don't believe it'll get cold. I mean, we're in the desert!"

It had already been hot that morning, as he and his father had packed up the car at home. They'd loaded in their backpacks, their tent, and two sleeping bags. Jason had sweated the whole time.

It was a long drive through the desert to Dad's favorite camping spot. Jason was excited to see the place where his dad had camped as a boy. He'd been hearing stories about it for his whole life. Dad's camping stories were the best.

"Just wait until we get out there," Dad had said as they drove deeper into the desert. "It's a beautiful place, especially when the sun is going down."

But they hadn't made it to the campsite. After they'd been driving for an hour or so, the car had suddenly started making noise. Then steam started coming out of the hood. All of a sudden, the car came to a screeching stop.

"Uh-oh," Dad had muttered. "This isn't good."

The car wouldn't start again, even though Dad kept trying. So Jason and his father had pushed it off the road onto the dusty shoulder.

Neither of their cell phones could pick up a signal.

"Do you think we should try to walk to town for help?" Jason asked. "We just drove through a town a while ago," he added. "I bet there's a gas station there at least."

Dad looked at the sky. "No," he said. "The sun will go down soon. It's too dangerous to start walking to town now. Legrand, the town we just drove through, is at least ten miles away. We wouldn't make it before sundown."

Jason asked, "What should we do?"

Dad shrugged. "We'll just have to set up camp here for the night," he said. "Tomorrow we'll walk to Legrand and find someone to fix the car. In the meantime, let's get settled. The sun will be down before you know it and it'll be cold out. We'll want to have our tent ready."

Jason didn't think the sun could set soon enough. It was so hot, and the sun beat down on him. He pulled off his T-shirt and wrapped it around his head. He thought that might help cool him off.

The spot where their car had broken down was a lonely place. It was flat and dusty and empty. All Jason could see for miles was the road they had been driving on. A small patch of woods was a few hundred yards off to the side. That was all.

"Okay," Dad said. He clapped his hands once. "Let's get this tent set up."

Jason groaned a little, but he got to his feet and went over to help his father. Dad showed Jason how to set up the tent. Soon it was ready.

"It looks pretty good!" Jason said.

"And just in time, too," Dad said. He squinted at the horizon to the west. "The sun is beginning to set," he added.

Jason hadn't noticed it, because he'd worked up a heavy sweat while setting up the tent. But Dad was right. The sun was sinking lower and lower. It was already getting much cooler.

"One more thing to do, and then we can relax for the night," Dad said. "Let's find some dry wood. We can make a campfire. Like I said, we'll be happy to have some heat in a little while."

Together, they walked over to the edge of the woods. There was a lot of dry wood, since many of the trees were dead. Jason and his dad each gathered an armful of wood. Then they walked back to the tent.

By the time they were back, it was getting dark.

About ten feet from the highway, Dad made a circle with small rocks. Then he showed Jason how to use the smaller twigs to get a small fire going inside the circle. Once there was a fire, Dad added a bunch of bigger sticks. Soon, a nice big campfire was blazing.

Jason sat down and relaxed. He hadn't realized how tired he was.

Dad leaned back on the rock with his hands behind his head. "Ahh," he said. "This is the life."

It was cooling off. With the campfire going, Jason had to admit camping was pretty nice. "It's not so bad out now," he said. He slipped his T-shirt back on.

"This reminds me of the last camping trip I took with my friends," Dad said. He leaned forward. His face was lit up by the crackling fire.

"Why, I bet I was about your age," Dad said. "Maybe a little older. Fifteen, maybe sixteen."

"Oh yeah?" Jason said. "Are you going to tell me about it?" His father told some great stories, but most of them were tall tales. They were full of close calls and amazing creatures.

"Yes," Dad said. He looked around. "As a matter of fact," he added, "I think we were at this very spot."

"Oh, come on," Jason replied with a laugh. "You're just making that up to trick me."

"No, it's true," Dad said. "You know I grew up in Legrand."

Jason nodded. "I know," he said.

"Well, my friends and I would walk to our campsite back in those days," Dad said. "And we didn't always camp in the same spot. Once, we camped right in those woods over there." He pointed to the woods where they'd collected sticks for the fire.

Jason stared over at the woods. "The forest looks pretty creepy in the dark," he said. A full moon was overhead. The woods had a silver light over them.

Dad nodded. "It sure does," he said. "Did back then, too."

Dad leaned back on the rock again. He tilted his hat down over his eyes.

"So, what happened?" Jason asked.

Dad said, "I better tell you exactly what happened on that camping trip. It was the reason we never went camping again."

CHAPTER 2

Dad's Tale

"It was a night a lot like tonight," Dad began. "The moon was full, and high in the sky. We didn't bring a tent. We had our campfire going, and we set up our sleeping bags around it."

"Was it cold that night?" Jason asked. "Like it is tonight?"

"It gets cold every night out here," Dad replied.

It really was cold. Jason started to climb into his sleeping bag.

"You're not ready to fall asleep yet, are you, Jay?" Dad asked.

"No," Jason replied. "I'm just chilly."

"Okay, good," Dad said. "You need to hear this whole story."

"I'll stay awake," Jason said.

"So," Dad continued, "we'd roasted some hot dogs, and we were lying around the fire in our sleeping bags. My friend Jimmy was a big joker. He'd just finished telling some goofy ghost stories."

"Sounds fun," Jason said.

"It was. We all had a good laugh," Dad went on, smiling, "and with all those hot dogs in our bellies, we got tired quick."

The fire popped and crackled. Jason lay on his back in his sleeping bag. He watched the orange embers float off, drifting up into the sky.

"Well, I must have fallen asleep at some point," Dad said. "Next thing I knew, I woke up. The fire had mostly died out."

"What woke you up?" Jason mumbled. He was getting pretty tired.

Dad shook his head. "To this day, I have no idea," he said. "But I was just going to roll over and go back to sleep when I heard this loud crack from deeper inside the woods."

Jason closed his eyes and pictured his father, as a boy his age, lying in his sleeping bag. It was hard to imagine his dad as a kid.

"Of course, after that, I was wide awake," Dad went on. "I sat up with a start. 'Guys,' I whispered to my friends. 'Guys!' But there was no reply. I went over to wake them up, thinking they had slept through the noise. But when I reached for Jimmy's sleeping bag, it was empty!"

Jason was getting very sleepy. He struggled to keep his eyes open. He focused on the embers floating above him.

"Max's sleeping bag was empty too. So was Sammy's," Dad went on. "Then I started to get a little scared, you know? My three friends had left the campsite in the middle of the night. Or they'd been taken!"

Jason imagined the empty sleeping bags and his dad as a boy, huddling alone by the dying fire. It was a creepy thought.

"Well," Dad continued, "I didn't like the idea of being out there all alone, so I started calling out for them. 'Jimmy! Max!' I called out. 'Sammy!' No reply. So I did what any kid alone would do. I grabbed a flashlight from my pack and went deeper into the woods, calling out their names. 'Jimmy! Max! Sammy!' But no one replied."

Jason could hardly stay awake. The images in his mind were swimming together, like a dream getting ready to start. He pictured his father lost in the woods. He pictured himself lost in the woods. He imagined a dying fire and three empty sleeping bags.

His dad kept telling the story. "About fifty yards into the woods, I saw something move," he said. "I yelled, 'Jimmy, is that you?' But of course there was no reply."

Dad paused. Then he said, "So I shined my flashlight where I'd seen the movement. And there, on the ground among the dry dead leaves, was Sammy's lucky red baseball hat. But Sammy, Jimmy, and Max were nowhere to be found." He stopped and took a deep breath.

"I had to find them, of course," Dad said. Jason barely heard him. "But at that moment, something — someone — bumped into me, and I dropped my flashlight. Everything went dark."

Jason didn't hear the rest of the story. He had fallen asleep.

CHAPTER 3

Awake

Jason felt like he'd only closed his eyes for a minute. The last thing he remembered was an image of his father as a boy. He had pictured his father holding a red baseball hat. Then Jason had closed his eyes.

The next thing he knew, he was awake again. The fire was dimmer, and he was cold. "Dad?" Jason mumbled, still groggy. "Did I fall asleep?" Dad didn't answer.

Dad must be asleep too, Jason thought. *I must have been sleeping for a little while. Dad probably got into his sleeping bag and went to sleep.*

Jason pulled the sleeping bag up over his head, rolled over, and closed his eyes. He started to fall asleep. Then, suddenly, he heard a noise.

Crack!

Jason shot up. "Dad!" he said. "Did you hear that? It sounded like it was coming from the woods!" But Dad didn't answer.

"Hey, Dad," Jason said, pushing off his sleeping bag. "Wake up, Dad."

Jason squinted into the darkness. He tried to see his father in the dim light of the dying fire.

He reached for his father's sleeping bag. "Dad," he said. He poked the sleeping bag. "I think someone's in the woods," Jason went on.

But Dad didn't answer. The sleeping bag was empty.

CHAPTER 4

Alone

Maybe he's in the tent, Jason thought. *He must be.*

Jason stuck his head into the tent. "Dad?" he said to the darkness. But the tent was empty too.

"Dad!" Jason called out. "Where did you go?"

Gradually, Jason's eyes became used to the darkness. That was a good thing. The light of the campfire was growing dimmer by the moment. Soon, it would be completely dark.

Jason stood by the fire. Thoughts raced through his mind. Had his dad left him there for some reason? Had something happened to his dad?

And why did it all seem so familiar?

Then he remembered. *My dream*, Jason thought. *I was dreaming about this, about my dad . . . and something about a red baseball hat, too.*

"Wait a second," Jason said out loud to himself. "That was no dream. It was Dad's story. The story of his last camping trip ever."

Jason peered into the night, toward the woods. "In the story, Dad went to the woods," he whispered.

But it was darker in the woods, Jason realized. *If I stay by the road,* he thought, *at least I might get help if someone drives by.*

He looked at the road and shivered. He remembered that even during the day, he hadn't seen any cars at all on this road. The chances of someone driving by at night seemed pretty slim.

"Then I guess I have no choice," Jason said. He reached into his bag and grabbed a flashlight. Then he said, "I have to go into the woods to find Dad."

He started walking away from the campsite. A few minutes later, Jason stepped into the forest.

He remembered that in the story, his dad had followed his friends into the woods. Jason took a deep breath and walked slowly into the woods.

"And then what?" Jason went on, struggling to remember. "What happened next?"

Suddenly, he heard a loud *Crack!*

"Who's there?" Jason called into the night. He spun to his right, and a shadow ran between the trees.

There was no reply. Jason shined his flashlight in every direction, but all he could see were tree trunks, more shadows, and branches.

"Dad, it's Jason," he yelled. "Where are you? Is this some kind of joke?"

Still, there was no reply.

In the chilling silence, Jason walked slowly toward the place where he thought he'd seen the shadow.

Crack!

Again, Jason spun around. Again, he saw a moving shadow.

"Dad! I'm scared," Jason pleaded into the night.

He ran toward the shadow. But it was dark, and he couldn't see the path. He also couldn't see the places where the path was covered with tree roots and plants. He had to just hope he wouldn't fall.

Just as he was about to catch up to the shadow, his foot caught on a tree root, and he fell, hard, onto the ground.

Jason sat down on the forest floor. There were dry branches and needles beneath him. He held on to his ankle.

It hurt a little, but he wasn't worried about that. He was worried about being lost. He had no idea where he was.

He tried to remember the rest of his dad's story.

"Why can't I remember?" Jason muttered. "What happened next? He ran into the woods, and then what?"

There was something about a red hat. "His friend's hat," Jason whispered.

The words seemed to echo through the forest and float back to him. "Dad's friend's hat," he whispered.

He remembered the image in his mind of his father. In the story, his father, a boy Jason's age, was kneeling in the woods. He was tightly holding on to a red baseball hat.

Jason shivered. *I need to keep moving*, he thought. *It's too cold to stay still.*

He reached down to push himself up from the ground. But his hand didn't touch the leaves and grass on the forest floor. Instead, it touched a hat. It was a big straw hat.

His father's straw cowboy hat.

Terrified, Jason stood up. He stared at the hat.

"Dad," he muttered. "I hope you're okay."

Just then, he began to remember the moment in the story when he'd fallen asleep.

Suddenly, something — or maybe someone — knocked into him. Jason's flashlight fell from his hand. The forest went dark.

CHAPTER 5

The Clearing

Moments later, Jason found himself lying on the ground. *I must have walked into a tree*, he thought.

His head felt dizzy. He felt around for his flashlight, but he couldn't find it.

"If only I'd been able to stay awake a little longer and hear the end of Dad's story," Jason said to himself as he stood up. "Then I'd know what's going on right now. Why am I such a baby?"

For a second, Jason thought about sitting back down on the cold forest ground. He felt like giving up.

"What's the point?" he said. "How can I find Dad in a pitch black forest?"

Just then, Jason saw a flash of light in the corner of his eye. A sliver of moonlight was glowing from a clearing not far away.

What's that light? he wondered. *Maybe Dad was heading over there.*

Jason walked quickly through the woods toward the ray of moonlight.

Soon he was standing on the edge of a clearing. There were no trees at all for at least a hundred yards. But right in the center of the big open area was a low, rocky hill.

Jason could see it clearly because of the bright light shining down from the full moon.

I'll head over and climb up the hill, Jason decided. Maybe from there, he'd be able to see his dad.

Jason easily made his way to the middle of the clearing. The moon was bright and high, and Jason's fears went away as he walked. In fact, he started to feel relaxed. The night was beautiful and the clearing was calm and peaceful.

Jason smiled. *When I find Dad,* he thought, *I'm going to tell him we should move our tent out here! This is awesome!*

But when Jason got close to the rocky hill, he realized it wasn't a hill at all. It was the mouth of a cave.

Jason peered into the opening. The mouth of the cave was dark, but Jason could tell the path in the cave went much farther than it looked from the outside.

"Wow," he said, peering into the cave. "It must go down pretty deep."

He looked around. The clearing was silent. "Dad," Jason called into the cave. "Are you in there?"

"In here . . . !" a voice replied.

"Dad!" Jason yelled. "Is that you?"

"That you . . . ?" came the reply.

Jason listened closely. He couldn't tell if he was hearing his father's voice, or just an echo of his own voice.

I'll just go in a little ways, he decided. *If it gets too dark, I'll turn around.*

Slowly, Jason started walking into the deep, dark tunnel. After only a few steps, it was so dark that Jason had to keep one hand on the cold cave wall. He didn't want to walk into anything.

He took slow, careful steps. The ground was a little slimy, and he slipped a couple of times.

Soon, his eyes became used to the darkness. And it almost seemed as if there was a light coming from deep inside the tunnel. He thought maybe there was another opening on the other side of the hill.

The tunnel began to slope down, though. Jason realized that he was going below the ground. But he kept on walking. He was still looking for his dad.

Jason kept going. He didn't have to keep a hand on the wall anymore, and after the first two hundred yards, the ground wasn't so slimy. But nothing else had changed, there was no sign of the other side of the tunnel, and he felt like he'd been walking for hours.

"And I haven't heard my father even once," he added to himself.

Jason tried calling out a couple of times, but only his echo came back. He was sure it was only his echo. He felt pretty stupid for thinking earlier that the echo had been his father's voice.

The cave went on and on. Just as Jason began to feel too tired to walk farther, he noticed something. It seemed as if the light was getting brighter as he walked down.

That didn't make sense. Jason didn't think he was in a tunnel anymore. Now, he was sure he was deep underground. He stopped to think. Should he turn around, or keep going?

Just then, Jason heard something. It was a scraping noise. It sounded like someone was scraping sticks against a rock. The sound was coming from somewhere to his left.

Jason squinted to the side. He had just been walking deeper into the cave. He had never stopped to look to the left or right before.

When he did stop, he saw that there was a hole in the wall right next to him. It looked like a small room, just off of the main path.

"I wonder how many rooms I missed," he whispered. "I might have walked right past dozens or hundreds of rooms in this cave!"

Suddenly he thought of something. Dad could have been in one of those rooms!

Carefully, Jason tiptoed into the little room. It was slightly brighter, and he could just make out a shape on the far side of the room.

"Is that you, Dad?" he said into the dim room. He reached out with his right hand, feeling for the wall. His fingers touched something sticky.

"Ew," Jason said. He quickly pulled his hand back. He squinted at his fingers and saw strands of some shiny, string-like stuff.

"Spider web," he said. "Gross."

Jason wiped his hand on his pants. Then he took another step, deeper into the chamber.

Hiss!

Jason stopped quickly. The hiss sounded like a snake. Was that possible? Could there be a snake in the cave?

Another hiss came out of the darkness, and a dark shape in front of Jason began to move.

It raised up off the ground, as if it was floating. In just a few seconds, it was towering over him.

Jason could see that there were eight skinny legs holding up the huge body.

Hiss!

Jason thought he might pass out, or throw up, or cry. Because standing right in front of him was a giant spider.

CHAPTER 6

Rich!

The huge beast hissed again. Jason heard its eight legs scratching on the stone floor. It was moving toward him.

As quickly as he could, Jason spun and ran back into the main hall.

He turned left, toward where the tunnel was getting lighter.

It was still really dark, though. Several times, Jason slipped or bumped his shoulder into the rock walls, hard.

He didn't stop running. He couldn't. He had to get away from the spider.

The tunnel curved sharply, and Jason fell into a small room on the side.

"Ow!" he yelled. Then he frowned. He had expected to land on hard, cold stone. But under him was something weird.

The ground seemed to shift and move beneath him. It felt strange and loose. There were some sharp edges, and some smooth ones.

Jason didn't know what was happening. He wanted to scream, but he was too afraid to do that.

He sat completely still and silent. He listened as the scratching noise of the giant spider's feet got louder and louder.

Jason held his breath.

A few seconds later, the sound started to get quieter. The spider was finally moving farther away. *Maybe it's heading back to its web,* Jason thought.

He reached down and touched the strange stuff he was sitting on. Then he picked up a handful of it. It was cold, and hard, and felt like metal. Some of the pieces felt like coins.

Squinting, Jason held the handful up to his face. The pieces shined in the low light and in his hands.

"Coins," he muttered. "And jewels!"

Jason jumped to his feet and looked around. The room he had stumbled into was filled with coins, jewels, and shining gold goblets.

"Treasure!" he shouted.

Jason ran through the room. He kicked at the coins, scooping up handfuls and tossing them into the air. He was laughing.

"Wait until Dad sees this!" he shouted. He'd forgotten, for a moment, that he had no idea where his father was.

Jason was happy. He hopped and jumped around the room.

Finally, he fell onto a heap of the shining riches. "Treasure!" he said, giggling. "It's all mine! All of this treasure belongs to me!"

"Ha!" came a thin, odd voice out of the darkness. Jason quickly stood up. Suddenly he didn't feel like laughing anymore.

"You think that is your treasure, young human?" the voice went on. "You'll never get that treasure. It belongs to me!"

A wicked laugh filled the room. Jason turned and looked around him. Nothing moved, except for a few coins that fell from his lap. He couldn't see anyone in the room.

"You want my treasure, human?" the voice went on.

It laughed an evil laugh. Then it said, "You can't have it. I haven't even decided if you can keep the one treasure you had when you entered this room."

"What treasure?" Jason asked in a trembling whisper.

The evil voice laughed again. Then it said, "Your life, of course!"

CHAPTER 7

Thief

"Who are you?" Jason shouted into the darkness. He peered around him. It was hard to see anything in the dim light of the treasure room.

"Too bad for you, young human thief," the laughing voice went on. "The treasure belongs to me. And I will keep it!"

Jason started to back out of the room. "I don't want your stupid treasure," he said.

But even as he said that, he was looking at the shining pile of coins and jewels. Glancing left and right, Jason quickly scooped up a handful of the gold and shoved it into his pocket.

"Ha ha ha!" the voice called from the darkness. "This treasure has been mine forever, and mine alone. Do not take that which you do not own!"

Jason started to run out of the room. "That which I do not own?" Jason whispered to himself as he ran. "Whoever that was, there's no way he could have seen me put those coins in my pocket."

Jason ran through the tunnel, keeping one hand on the wall.

Besides, Jason thought as he ran. *Why would someone with that much treasure miss a few little coins?*

Jason panted as he ran up the tunnel. His footsteps echoed as they pounded against the floor. Once, he thought he heard the giant spider hiss, but he didn't stop long enough to look back. He just kept running, listening only to his breath and the evil laughter from behind him.

"This treasure has been mine forever and mine alone," the voice screamed down the tunnel. "Do not take that which you do not own! Be sure what you have is all your own, or you'll always be here and made of stone!"

Jason's feet thundered on the hard floor. He heard the coins jingle in his pockets.

Jason didn't know much about treasure or gold, but he knew jewels and coins were worth money — a lot of money. That dumb spider didn't need a few golden coins.

The tunnel felt longer on the way out, even though he was running instead of walking slowly. For a moment, Jason thought he must have gone the wrong way.

Then he forgot about feeling lost, because the evil voice filled the tunnel. "The grown-up human did not get my treasure tonight, you know," the voice said. "And his friends did not get it thirty years ago."

CHAPTER 8

Three Pieces

"Thirty years ago?" Jason muttered. "Who cares about thirty years ago?"

Suddenly, Jason realized what the voice meant. He stopped running. Thirty years ago was when his dad had been there, at the same place, with his friends.

"And thirty years ago must be when his story took place," Jason muttered to himself.

Suddenly, the voice rang out again: "Do not take that which you do not own!"

Jason looked down at the stolen treasure in his palm. With a deep breath, he turned around and called into the chamber, "Here!"

He heaved the coins down the tunnel. For a moment, he stood and listened to the clink of gold coins on stone. The sounds echoed a few seconds. Then they stopped. The cave was silent.

Jason sighed. "I guess we'll never be rich," he whispered. Then he turned and walked slowly up the tunnel toward the moonlight.

But the voice wasn't done. "Jingle, jangle, jewels and gold," the voice said. "Three pieces still gone. He won't grow old."

"Three pieces?" Jason said. He dug deep into his pockets, but they were empty.

"I gave it all back!" Jason called into the darkness below. "I don't have anything left!"

He waited for the voice to say something in reply, but there was only silence. "Okay then," Jason muttered. He stepped out of the cave into the moonlight.

But when he got outside, Jason saw a figure near the entrance. When he walked a little closer, he realized it was a life-sized stone statue of a man.

Jason stepped up to the statue. "That's funny," he said, looking at it. "I don't remember seeing a statue on the way in. I must have gone in a different tunnel. Guess I did make a wrong turn after all."

Jason moved in for a closer look. He walked slowly around the statue. Then he peered up at the stone face. "Weird," he said. "It looks like . . ."

A wicked laugh cut him off. "Ha ha ha!"

Jason spun toward the opening to the cave. No one was there. "Jingle, jangle, jewels and gold," the voice called. "Three pieces still gone, so he'll not grow old."

"I gave back all the gold!" Jason shouted.

The voice laughed. "Be sure all you have is all your own," the evil voice said, "or you'll always be here, made of stone."

"Made of stone?" Jason said. He glanced up at the statue's face. "It can't be," he said. But it was. "Dad!" Jason screamed. "Dad!"

CHAPTER 9

The Statue

"Wake up, Dad!" Jason shouted at the statue.

"He'll always be here," the voice whispered. The whisper echoed through the forest. Then the voice said, "He's made of stone."

"You did this?" Jason said. He spun around to face the cave. "Why?"

"Three pieces still gone!" the voice replied, laughing madly.

Jason felt like he was going to pass out. He sat down on the ground and put his head in his hands. But as he stared down at the ground, he saw something shiny. Three gold coins lay on the dirt. Jason picked them up.

"Here!" he shouted, facing the cave. "Take your stupid gold!" He tossed the coins into the cave.

The voice was silent for a few moments. Then it said, "What's yours is yours, what's mine is mine. Now mine is back with me, and yours is fine."

Suddenly, the statue crumpled to the ground in a heap. The voice chuckled, then faded away into silence.

"Dad!" Jason said, dropping to his knees beside his father. "Are you okay?"

"Where am I?" Dad asked.

"Outside that cave," Jason said. "You were . . . he turned you into a statue."

Jason helped his father to his feet. Dad nodded as he brushed the dirt from his pants and shirt. "I remember now," he said. He shook his head. "I was a fool, wasn't I?" he said quietly.

"What do you mean?" Jason asked. He and his father started to walk back through the forest.

"I thought he wouldn't notice just three coins," Dad explained. "After you'd fallen asleep, I thought I'd just run down here, grab a couple of coins, and run back."

"But why?" Jason asked. "We don't need three gold coins that badly!"

Dad shrugged. He put his arm around Jason's shoulders. "I just wanted to show you that my story was true," Dad explained.

Jason smiled and said, "You showed me it was true all right!"

Dad laughed. "I guess I did!" he said.

Jason added, "Now I'll tell you about the giant spider!"

About the Author

Steve Brezenoff lives in St. Paul, Minnesota with his wife, Beth, and their small, smelly dog, Harry. Besides writing books, he enjoys playing video games, riding his bicycle, and helping middle-school students to improve their writing skills. Steve's ideas almost always come to him in dreams, so he does his best writing in his pajamas.

About the Illustrator

Richard Pellegrino is a professional illustrator who lives and works in Warwick, Rhode Island. His work has been published by CMYK, Night Shade Books, Compass Press, and Tale Bones Press. He is also an accomplished figurative painter and has shown his oil paintings in numerous galleries across the United States.

Glossary

campsite (KAMP-site)—the place where a tent is set up for camping

clearing (KLEER-ing)—an area of a forest or woods where trees have been removed

echo (EK-oh)—when a sound echoes, it repeats because its sound waves have met a large surface and have bounced back

embers (EM-burz)—the hot, glowing remains of a fire

familiar (fuh-MIL-yur)—if you are familiar with something, you know it well

groggy (GROG-ee)—sleepy or dizzy

statue (STACH-oo)—a model of a person made from a solid material

thief (THEEF)—someone who steals things

treasure (TREZH-ur)—gold, jewels, money, or other valuable things that were collected

tunnel (TUHN-nuhl)—a passage built underground

Discussion Questions

1. Who did the creepy voice in the cave belong to?

2. Why was Dad turned into a statue?

3. What happened in this book that was like the story that Dad told Jason?

Writing Prompts

1. Jason never heard the end of his dad's story before he fell asleep. Write out what you think happened in Dad's story.

2. If you found treasure, what would you do with it?

3. What do you think happened to Dad between when Jason fell asleep and when he was turned into a statue? Write the story of Dad's night.

Internet Sites

Do you want to know more about subjects related to this book? Or are you interested in learning about other topics? Then check out FactHound, a fun, easy way to find Internet sites.

Our investigative staff has already sniffed out great sites for you!

Here's how to use FactHound:

1. Visit *www.facthound.com*

2. Select your grade level.

3. To learn more about subjects related to this book, type in the book's ISBN number: **9781434207951**.

4. Click the **Fetch It** button.

FactHound will fetch the best Internet sites for you!